W9-AUD-438

First published in 1992 by Éditions MILAN
300, rue Léon-Joulin 31101 Toulouse Cedex 100—France

Published in the United States in 1997 by Silver Press,
A Division of Simon and Schuster,
299 Jefferson Road
Parsippany, NJ 07054

Printed in Belgium by Casterman, S.A., Tournai
10 9 8 7 6 5 4 3 2 1

Library of Congress Cataloging-in-Publication Data

Chausse, Sylvie.
[Héritage de l'oncle MacLaughton. English]
The Egg and I/by Sylvie Chausse;
illustrated by François Crozat.
p. cm.

Summary: When his uncle dies and leaves Matthew only the
order to "go cook an egg," the results are astounding.

ISBN 0-382-39286-8 (LSB)—ISBN 0-382-39284-1(PBK)

[1. Inheritance and succession—Fiction. 2. Dinosaurs—Fiction. 3. Zoos—Fiction.]
I. Crozat, Franáois, ill. II. Title.
PZ7.C3972In 1997
95-36014 [Fic]—dc20
CIP AC

The EGG and I

Story by Sylvie Chausse
Illustrations by François Crozat

Silver Press
Parsippany, New Jersey

Uncle McLaughton rested in his big canopied bed. He did not feel very well. To warm up his old bones, his housekeeper had prepared six hot water bottles. But this didn't help. The wind was blowing so hard on the Highlands, and it was so cold in the huge room of the Scottish mansion, that he continued to shiver. Neither the goose down quilt nor the hot cocoa in the silver pot helped him.

So he had the notary come who, without taking off his mittens, wrote as Uncle McLaughton dictated his will.

Scotch
WHISKY

“I, Conrad McLaughton, having reached the ripe old age of 108, give to my nephew Edward my mansion, the paintings, and the furniture. To his wife, Marilou, I give all the jewelry, the contents of the chests, and the trinkets.

“To my nephew Arthur, who is the strongest, I leave the weapons and the armor. As for my nephew Matthew, the good-for-nothing, he should go cook an egg.”

And with these words, Conrad McLaughton died.

The day of the funeral, all the nephews were there. Marilou couldn't stop crying; she had hidden a big onion in her handkerchief.

Arthur looked sad; he was going to miss a football game he wanted to see.

Edward's forehead was wrinkled with worry; he was hoping his share of the inheritance would cover the cost of his plane ticket.

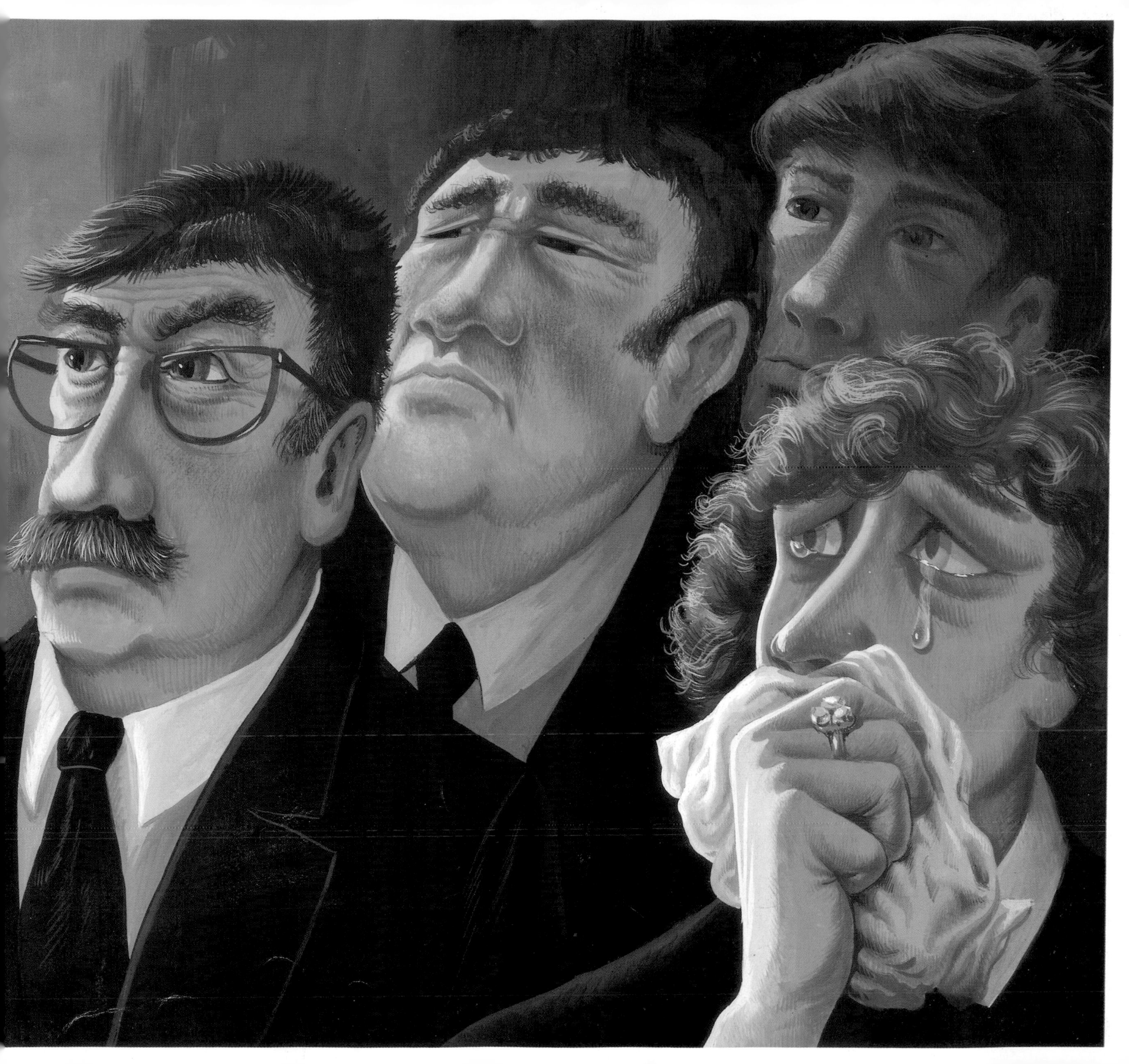

Matthew was sad. He didn't know his old uncle very well, but he regretted he had not arrived earlier to cheer him up a little.

At the end of the funeral ceremony, all four went to the notary's office. They no longer felt the cold in their feet; they were waiting for the good news. Arthur was delighted; the weapons and armor would be his! He and his friend would be able to organize great tournaments as in the olden days. Marilou pictured herself covered with precious stones, wearing ruffled dresses, and making her friends jealous. Edward was the happiest. With the sale of the mansion, the paintings, and the furniture, he would be able to buy a private jet.

Matthew, however, felt sad. Why did Uncle Conrad call him a good-for-nothing? It was true that his life had been less successful than his cousins. He was only a zookeeper—not really a job where you can get rich.

They all went back to the mansion to divide up everything. Marilou wanted to help herself first, but the chests were empty, the trimmings on the dresses were moth-eaten and the lace was ripped. Even worse, the jewelry was fake—cheap junk!

Arthur wanted to grab the set of weapons hanging in the great room, but they were so rusted that at the slightest touch, they crumbled to dust. The armor also fell apart, and colonies of mice who lived there escaped squeaking.

Edward smiled. He, at least, had inherited something solid. But very quickly, the notary disillusioned him: before selling the mansion, it would be necessary to redo the roof, fix the walls, and repair the crumbling tower. As for the paintings, they were the work of Conrad McLaughton himself and were only poor scribblings.

So the three cousins headed back to the airport. Marilou no longer needed the onion to make her cry, Arthur wanted to hurry back to find out who won the football game, and Edward was upset at the idea of paying for his return ticket.

Only Matthew remained at the mansion. He was no longer sad. He figured that Uncle McLaughton had been a practical joker!

"Sir," said the notary, "the will says that you must cook an egg. This clause must be honored."

Matthew thought this very odd, but as it happened, he was hungry and would have loved a bacon omelette.

The housekeeper threw up her hands: "For some time, Mr. McLaughton had been eating only biscuits dipped in hot cocoa, and the closest grocery store is five miles away. What are we going to do?"

The butler had an idea. “There has been,” he said, “for years and years, a huge egg in the arched cave. My great-grandfather, who was the butler for the McLaughtons then, had heard them say that it had always been in the same spot, and the mansion had been built around it without moving it.”

They went into the cave. There, between two rows of casks, they found an enormous egg, all gray, with a shell as hard as a stone. It took the three of them to carry it back up the narrow stairs.

The housekeeper was pulling her hair out; she had neither a stove not a pot large enough to cook it—even the laundry basin would be too small!

Matthew had an idea: "Let's stir up the fire in the huge fireplace and put the egg in the flames."

So they rolled the egg into the fire, so it could cook. This took a great effort. Of course, it would take longer than the usual three minutes to cook this egg!

After almost an hour, they heard strange noises coming from inside the egg and noticed that the shell was beginning to crack. Matthew already had put on his napkin.

But all at once, in a single stroke, the top of the egg was pushed up and a strange head, like that of an enormous lizard turned toward them.

The housekeeper screamed, the notary fainted, and the butler turned as yellow as the stripes of his vest.

Matthew recognized that it was a baby dinosaur because he was familiar with all kinds of animals, and he had no fear of this strange creature. He was right not to be afraid because this was a gigantic baby who had been waiting thousands of years for the heat that would allow him to hatch and who only asked for kindness and a few tons of fresh grass

There was plenty of fresh grass at the zoo where Matthew worked. So he reassured the housekeeper, consoled the butler, and shook the notary to wake him up.

Then, after everyone had come to their senses and had eaten some of Uncle's biscuits soaked in hot cocoa, Matthew took away the prehistoric monster—now called Médor—who followed him with tearful eyes of love.

In the zoo's garden, after an understandable panic, everyone surrounded Matthew asking questions and congratulating him.

But Matthew wanted above all to take care of his new pet. He put him very near the elephant, so he would have company, brought him tender grass, and patted his enormous scaly head.

What success! Each day hundreds of visitors squeezed into the zoo, and on Sunday they came at dawn, waiting in front of the gates with sandwiches and thermos bottles. Before long, everyone rushed toward the enclosure where Médor grazed calmly.

When the gigantic animal was compared to the elephant, the elephant seemed no larger than a poodle. Médor would lie on his back so that Matthew, perched on his big stomach, could tickle him with the help of a rake, making Médor wriggle and sigh with pleasure. It was a triumph, it was wild!

People shouted, they marveled, they clapped. Everyone threw peanuts and small coins.

And each evening, when he came to put Médor to bed, Matthew collected the money and put it into big bags. Soon he was so rich that he bought the zoo and built a place for Médor as big as a cathedral.

Later, Matthew bought the mansion from Edward as well as the paintings and the furniture. From Marilou he bought the jewels, the contents of the chests, and all the trinkets. From Arthur he bought all the weapons and armor.

After this, he called the masons, the carpenters, the painters, and the roofers. He had all of the trimmings stitched back on the dresses, and the weapons and armor melted and recast.

Soon the castle was like new. The housekeeper and the butler could hardly believe it: you would think you were back in the good old days.

As for the collection of Uncle McLaughton's paintings, Matthew added three magnificent portraits that he painted during his long vacation spent in the field where the dinosaur feasted on the green grass: one of himself, one of Médor, and one of the old joker McLaughton.

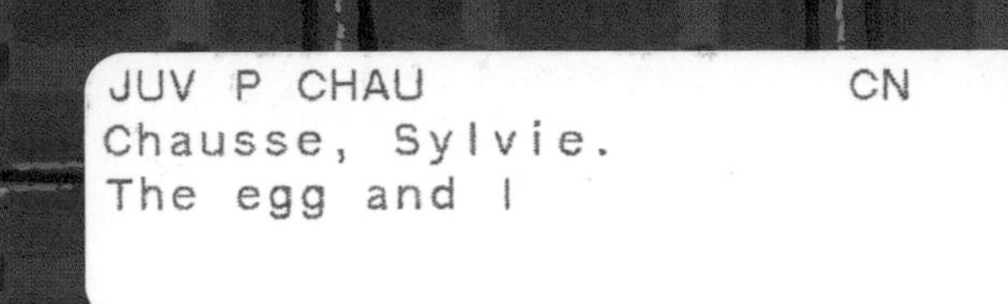
Ex-Library: Friends of
Lake County Public Library